I Was
a Third Grade
Spy

I Was a
Third Grade
SPY

by Mary Jane Auch

illustrated by
Herm Auch

Holiday House / New York

Library of Congress Cataloging-in-Publication Data
Auch, Mary Jane.
I was a third grade spy / by Mary Jane Auch ; illustrated by Herm Auch.—1st ed.
p.   cm.
Summary: When Brian's dog, Arful, suddenly begins talking,
Brian and his two friends send the dog to find out what their classmates
are planning for the school talent show.
ISBN 0-8234-1576-7 (hardcover)
[1. Dogs—Fiction. 2. Talent shows—Fiction. 3. Schools—Fiction.] I. Auch,
Herm, ill. II. Title.

PZ7.A898 Iad 2001
[Fic]—dc21   00-058060

to Barbara Bergh and
Carolyn Baer

chapter

1

Today was my first day of school and could have been my last. People do weird things in school. My friend Brian says he loves school because he learns a lot of stuff there. Well, I guess he's right. When I stepped into the school I couldn't talk, and now I can.

It all started a couple of weeks ago when Brian got this idea of trying to make me think I was a cat. A cat! Is there anything in this world I hate more than cats? I don't think so! I am Arful Lewis, one hundred percent dog and proud of it. I am honest, loyal, and trustworthy, all of which cats are not. They're mean and sneaky. Period. End of story!

Anyway, Brian and his buddies, Josh and Dougie, were trying to turn me into a cat with this hyp . . . hypno . . . something or other. Brian swung a sparkly thing in front of my nose and kept saying I was getting sleepy. Well, that worked, because I never have any trouble going to sleep. I've even done it standing up. But just as I started to doze off each time, Brian would tell me I was turning into a cat.

I wouldn't be caught dead turning into a cat, but something funny happened to Josh. He was the one holding me while Brian did the hypno business. Right after that, Josh started sending out these sneaky cat vibes. I was the only one who noticed at first. That's probably because dogs are especially sensitive to cat vibes. Anyway, Josh kept getting more and more catlike over the next three weeks until the night of the Science Fair.

That's what all the fuss was about. The kids took me to this place in the school called a stage. There were bright lights that hurt my eyes. Brian had told me about ten times to behave myself, so I sat quietly even though other people's pets were being real pains. There were a couple of dogs running around, and somebody had a bird who flew up to a pole above the stage and kept yelling "pretty bird." Birds can be so stuck on themselves. So they can fly, big deal! Give me a pair of wings and I'll fly, too.

Anyway, when it was our turn at the Science Fair, Brian just read this long boring report about how I was doing cat things. I was not! I would have told everybody, but I didn't know how to human-talk yet, even though I had always understood most human words.

Pretty soon I saw those dogs sniffing the air, and I could tell they were picking up those cat vibes from Josh. Before I could stop them, they chased Josh clear out of the school. Luckily, the dogs didn't make it through the door, but the rest of us ran after Josh and found him up in a tree.

Dougie was the one who figured out that Josh had been hypnotized. He coaxed Josh down from the tree and started swinging this dangly thing in front of his nose, just like Brian had done with me. He kept telling Josh that he was a boy, not a cat. He had to hurry, because Brian's mother and the princi-pal had come out of the school and were looking for us. I was watching that swinging thing real close, getting a little sleepy.

Then, when Dougie snapped his fingers, Josh was himself again. And that's the exact moment that I

knew how to human-talk. I remember Josh said he
was hungry.

Then I said, "I want a pepperoni pizza."

They all stared at me, then Brian grabbed my collar. "Lets run for those bushes before anyone sees
us. We have to figure out what just happened before
Mom and Mr. Purvis get here."

chapter

When Arful started talking, I didn't have any idea what was going on. I wasn't even sure how I got outside.

"C'mon, Josh," Dougie said, grabbing my wrist. Brian had hold of Arful's collar, and we all ran through the darkness and dove into the hollow space under some bushes.

"What's happening?" I asked, pulling away from Dougie. "Who are we running from?"

Brian pushed me farther under the bush. "Quiet, Josh," he whispered. "I'll explain in a minute. Mom and Mr. Purvis are coming this way."

"I don't think the boys are around here,"

Mr. Purvis said. "Are you sure you saw them come outside?"

Mrs. Lewis's voice came from right next to the bush. I could see her feet. "Brian always comes when I call him. I guess I was mistaken. They must be in the building after all."

Their voices grew fainter as they walked back to the school. "Okay, the coast is clear," Brian said. We crawled out from our hiding place.

"Will somebody please tell me why we were hiding?" I asked.

"It's because of Arful," Dougie said. "We think he can talk."

"Of course I can talk," Arful said. "I've always talked, but you never listened before."

Brian patted Arful. "Your talking is different now, Arful. You're speaking like a human."

Arful's eyes grew wide. "I am? Who do I sound like?"

"He really is talking!" I said. I couldn't believe my ears.

Dougie pounded me on the back so hard I almost fell over. "This is so cool! A talking dog! Arful is going to be famous. He'll make us *all* famous!"

"Everybody be quiet!" Brian ordered. "We need to be scientific about this. We have to keep Arful's talking secret until we can figure out what happened. Josh, remember how you were the one to hold Arful when we were hypnotizing him into thinking he was a cat?"

"I never thought I was a cat," Arful mumbled.

Brian patted him again. "No, you didn't, Arful, but it worked on Josh."

"What do you mean?" I asked. "I thought I was a cat? That's ridiculous."

"You did, Josh," Dougie said. "Just before I hypnotized you back, you thought you had a tail."

"I did not." I looked over my shoulder.

Then I remembered something about being afraid of dogs and liking fish.

"See?" Dougie grinned. "You did think you were a cat, Josh. You'd still be sharpening your nails on that tree if I didn't hypnotize you into being a kid again."

My fingernails were just sore enough to make me believe him. I could feel my face go red. I wondered what other stupid things I had done as a cat.

"And since Dougie didn't have a clue what he was doing," Brian said, "he hypnotized Arful into thinking he's a kid. Remember how you were scared of dogs when you thought you were a cat?"

"Yeah, I was," I said. "That's weird."

Brian pushed his glasses up on his nose. "Well, maybe now that Arful thinks he's a kid, he likes cats."

"Me like cats? Are you nuts?" Arful pulled himself up to his full height. "I'm a dog! Not a kid, not a cat. I'm a D-O-G. Got that? And I do not—repeat, NOT—like C-A-T-S!"

"Wow," Dougie breathed. "He can spell, too. Is this awesome, or what? We should enter him in a spelling bee."

"Wait!" I said. "If Arful is really talking, we have to protect him. We can't let anybody know about this."

"Why not?" Dougie whined. "This is the best thing that ever happened to me in my whole life." He grabbed for Arful's collar. "C'mon. Let's take him into the school and show everybody what he can do."

I put both arms around Arful so Dougie couldn't get him. "This didn't happen to you, Dougie. It happened to Arful. And if you tell people about it, they'll take him away from Brian so they can do testing on him."

"Yeah?" Dougie countered. "Well, I bet they'll pay tons of money for him. Brian will be rich. And he'll probably share it with us. Especially me, since I'm the one who hypnotized Arful into talking."

"I don't want to be rich," Brian said. "I want to keep my dog. Nobody's giving up his secret."

"Thanks, Brian," Arful said. And his tail thumped the ground.

chapter 3

The kids are all upset about me being able to talk. You'd think they'd be happy. Now they know I actually understand what Brian is telling me to do. Of course that doesn't mean I'm going to do it.

They have this big argument about what to do with me, but they finally get it settled.

"Okay," Brian says. "We have to sneak back into the school and pretend we were there the whole time. We can say we were in the boys' bathroom. And nobody says anything about Arful being able to talk. Is that clear?"

"Does that mean me, too?" I ask. "I can't tell anybody?"

"That means *especially* you!" Brian says.

"Well, can I at least tell your mother I don't like that new Veggi-Pooch dog food?"

Josh squats down and puts his arm around my neck. "Don't you understand, Arful? You can't say anything."

I still can't see what the problem is. "I wasn't going to tell her about the talking," I explain. "I just wanted to tell her about the dog food. It's really yucky." I shiver just thinking about it. Mrs. Lewis is always trying to feed me stuff that's healthy. I'll eat almost anything, but feeding Veggi-Pooch to your dog should be against the law!

Brian pulls out his notebook. "Very interesting." He writes something down and closes the book. "Arful may be talking like a kid, but he's still thinking like a dog."

Why would thinking like a dog be a problem? I've been doing it all my life, and it worked fine until I started talking like a kid. If you ask me, the kid-talking is the problem, not the dog-thinking.

chapter
4

I don't know why school can't just be simple. You go in the morning, you learn a few new facts, and you go back home in the afternoon. Oh, sure, they should have neat stuff like art and music. Gym, lunch, and recess are good, too. But if you ask me, trying to make school exciting by setting up a competition is just asking for trouble. I mean the Science Fair last Friday night almost ruined my life. So on Monday morning when Mr. Purvis announced that the school talent contest would be in one week, I wanted to run screaming out of the room.

"I can't believe it," I said as Brian and I walked home from school Monday afternoon. "We just got over the Science Fair. My mom still doesn't believe

SIGN UP NOW

TALENT SHOW

OCTOBER 7

ASTOUND YOUR FRIENDS

that we were in the boys' bathroom while every-body was looking for us. And how long do you think it will be before Arful blurts something out in front of people? He's like a bomb ready to explode. I'm amazed that we made it through the weekend."

"Arful understands about not talking," Brian said. "I've explained to him how important it is."

"He's a dog, Brian. We don't know what's going on in that head of his."

Just then Dougie caught up to us. "I know what you guys are doing. You're thinking up something for the talent show, right?"

"Wrong," I said. "We're having a discussion about Arful."

"What about Arful?" Dougie asked, grinning. "Has he said anything interesting lately?"

Brian grabbed his arm. "Shhhh! You want some-body to find out about him talking?"

Dougie shook loose. "Relax, will you? There's nobody around to hear. I'm not giving away your secret. But I do think we should do something for the talent show. If it's even half as much fun as the Science Fair, we'll have a blast."

"Mr. Purvis said the talent show was optional," I said. "That means they can't force you into enter-ing it if you don't want to. Especially if you don't have any talent."

Dougie's grin disappeared. "Who says I don't have any talent?"

"I never said that. I'm the one with no talent. You and Brian can do anything you want. I'll be out in the audience clapping my head off for you."

Brian had that "I'm coming up with another humiliating idea" look on his face. "We need something spectacular . . . like tightrope walking."

"You get dizzy standing on the second rung of a ladder," I reminded him.

"It could be a low tightrope."

Dougie snorted. "Oh, yeah, that would be exciting. We could just put the rope on the floor and see if you could walk in a straight line without losing your balance."

Dougie had hit a sore spot. Brian might be the class brain, but he was the most uncoordinated kid I'd ever met. That also ruled out Brian's next three suggestions, which were Irish step dancing, gymnastics, and a skateboard demonstration.

"I've always wanted to do a magic act," Brian offered, picking up steam again. "I could pull a rabbit out of a hat. Or maybe I could saw somebody in half."

"You're not getting near me with a sharp instrument," Dougie said.

I shook my head. "Me neither. I don't care what you come up with. I'm not getting up on stage and making a fool of myself again."

I started walking faster, but Brian grabbed the back of my shirt. "Wait! That was different. You weren't yourself at the Science Fair."

Dougie snorted. "That's for sure. He was a cat,

for Pete's sake. Hey, Josh, maybe your talent could be catching mice."

I ignored him.

Dougie suddenly smacked himself in the head. "Duh! I know what our talent is. We can win this thing for sure, because we have a secret weapon. It's Arful."

"Arful is our talent?" Brian looked puzzled.

"Dougie," I said, "go home and look up talent in the dictionary. If it says a talent has four legs and barks, then you're right. We have a talent."

"Don't mess with me, Josh. If it weren't for me you'd be using a litter box by now. We have a talking dog. How talented is that?"

"That's Arful's talent, not ours!" I said. "And you know we can't let anybody know about it. First thing you know, we'd have reporters coming in here and then Arful would be off in Hollywood making movies."

Dougie shook his head. "I still don't see what's wrong with that."

Brian spoke up. "I won't let it happen. I want to hypnotize him back to normal right now."

"No!" Dougie yelled. "Please, Brian. Arful is a scientific miracle. You don't want to mess that up, do you?"

"It's like an experiment," I added. "We'll be the first humans to learn what goes on in a dog's mind."

Brian thought for a minute, then nodded. We had won him over. Brian could never resist a scientific experiment.

chapter 5

There's a park on the corner of our street where I wait every day for Brian to come home from school. I used to wait right outside the school, but they made me stop doing that because I couldn't remember not to bark. It's just that I would think of something to tell Brian, and I'd bark it out right then. It didn't work, though, because human ears aren't very good, and Brian didn't understand dog-talk anyway.

Now everything is different. For the first time, I can talk when I run over to meet them. "Hi, guys! Wanna play stick?"

Brian puts his hand over my muzzle. "Shhh! Didn't I tell you not to talk in public?"

I shake Brian's hand loose. "What's public? Is this public?"

"Anyplace where other people can hear you is public." Brian looks around. "Did you say anything to the guy sitting over there reading on the bench?"

"You mean the man who has a German shepherd at home and had eggs for breakfast?"

"You were talking with him?" Brian drops to his knees and puts his arm around my neck. This is not a hug.

"No, not exactly," I say, pulling away. "He has German shepherd scent on his pant legs and eggshell scent on his fingers, also rye toast. He cooks his own breakfast."

Dougie sits on the ground next to me. "That's awesome, buddy. You can tell all that stuff by smell? What can you tell about me?"

"Well," I begin. "Your shirt tells me what you did all weekend. Saturday morning you ate some fried—"

"If he starts talking about your smells, we'll be here all night," Josh says. "Let's get out of here. Here comes Emily Venable."

"Oh, no," Brian moans.

"Emily has a crush on you, Brian," Dougie says in a high voice like a girl.

Brian grabs me by the collar, but we're too late to

get away. Funny, this girl doesn't look big enough to crush anybody, but I'll keep an eye on her just in case.

"Hi, Brian! Have you thought of something to do for the talent show next Monday night?"

"We're working on it." Brian keeps his eyes on me and puts his finger to his lips. I know that means no barking. I wonder if it means no talking, too. Probably not. Sit and stay each have their own signs. No talking must have one, too.

The girl laughs. It's a nasty laugh. I let my lip curl up a little just to let her know who's boss. "You're working with these two again?" she asks. "Wasn't the Science Fair humiliating enough for you?"

I don't know what humiliating means, but I can tell she hurt Brian's feelings. I don't like this girl. "You're not a nice person," I say.

The girl's head spins toward Josh and me. Josh steps in front of me. "You're being mean to my friends," I say, peering around his knees.

The girl makes a face. "Sticks and stones may break my bones—"

"Stick?" I ask. "You wanna play stick?" Funny, she doesn't look like the stick-playing type.

Dougie grabs the stick and talks in a low voice. He sounds sort of like me. "Wanna play stick, buddy? Come on. Let's go." He runs off and I follow, keeping my eye on that stick the whole time. But Dougie doesn't want to play stick at all. He stops close by and pretends to be petting me. I can tell he's trying to hear what the girl is saying to Brian.

"You're all weird," she says. "You couldn't come up with an act for the talent show if your lives depended on it. I'm planning to do something with Lissa Franken and Cara Leone and we're going to win."

23

"Oh, yeah?" Josh says.

The girl looks at him through little slit eyes—just like a cat's. Makes the hair on my back bristle. "I don't think you have any ideas at all."

"Well, that's where you're wrong, Emily," Josh says. "We just happen to have a great act and we're going to win."

"Now we're in trouble," Dougie whispers.

"And just to let you know how sure we are of winning," Brian says, "you girls get to order us around in school for a whole week if we lose."

Dougie groans. "Now we're in *big* trouble."

The girl smiles, but it's not a happy smile. It's mean, like a cat. "Deal! And if we lose, you get to order us around." She turns to leave, then looks over her shoulder. "Of course that won't happen, because we're not going to lose."

We all watch as she walks away. If that girl had a tail, it would have been twitching, the way a cat struts right after she's swatted some poor unsuspecting dog. I smell trouble.

chapter 6

After the bet with Emily, Brian kept coming up with more useless ideas for our talent show act. His final plan was off the wall. After school on Tuesday, he had us dress up as girls, using his mother's old wigs and clothes from a trunk in their attic. We were supposed to lip-synch a song from one of her old CDs. When we looked at ourselves in the mirror, we almost fell over laughing. At first Arful seemed spooked by the way we looked. He stayed in the corner, growling at us, as if he couldn't figure out who we were. Then he must have caught our scent, because he finally calmed down and fell asleep.

"This is perfect," Brian said. He had on a long blond wig and was wearing a bright orange, short dress. With his skinny legs sticking out of the bottom, he looked like a popsicle with hair.

Dougie could have been a clone of the Good Witch of the East from Oz with a bright red, puffy wig and a ruffled, pink prom dress. He had tried to put on some sticky false eyelashes, but one was stuck to his eyebrow and the other was flapping off the ends of his own lashes. He twirled around the room until he tripped over his sneaker laces.

I felt ridiculous in a slinky purple dress, and even more ridiculous when Brian plopped on my head a

brown curly wig that was too big and almost covered my eyes. "You look great," he said. "We almost don't need to have an act at all. If we just stand on the stage in these outfits, we'll win for sure."

Dougie stopped dead. "Stand on the stage? Looking like this? People would still remember this when we're seniors in high school. They'd have pictures in the yearbook."

"I know!" Brian said, admiring his reflection. "Great, huh?"

Dougie put his hands on Brian's shoulders. One last blink sent the eyelash sliding down his cheek like a wounded centipede. "Not great. We'd never live this down. It's okay for messing around in your attic, but if you think I'm going out in public like this, you're crazy."

Brian turned to me. "Okay, then Josh and I will do it, right, Josh?"

I wrestled myself out of the stretchy purple dress. "Wrong!" I tossed the wig into the trunk but missed. It skimmed right past Arful's nose. He woke up and dove for the wig. He grabbed it in his teeth and shook it, then he let it drop to the floor. "Don't worry, kids," he said. "Whatever that thing was, it can't hurt you now. I just killed it."

After school on Wednesday we had an emergency meeting in Brian's new treehouse.

Brian pulled out his notebook. "Since we can't come up with any ideas on our own, we need a new strategy. If we know what the girls are planning, we can come up with something better."

Dougie caught my eye and we both shook our heads. Arful was sleeping in a patch of sunshine on the floor.

"All right," Brian said, "listen up. I heard the girls say they were meeting this afternoon in Emily's playhouse to work on their act."

I looked out the window. Emily lived on the next street over, just a couple of houses down from Brian's. "We can see who goes in from here."

Brian pushed up his glasses. "That's not good enough. We need to know what they're talking about. We have to send in a spy."

Dougie moaned. "Oh, no. You're not sending me in there."

"Relax," I said. "They wouldn't let you in there."

"Josh is right," Brian said. "They wouldn't let any of us in there. That's why we're sending Arful."

Arful woke up when he heard his name. "You're sending me where?"

"To spy on the girls," Dougie said.

Arful wrinkled his nose. "I don't like girls. They have a sickening, soapy smell. It's enough to make me throw my biscuits."

Dougie grinned. "You mean toss your cookies?"

"Whatever," Arful said. "But you guys always smell great, especially you, Dougie." He sniffed the soles of Dougie's sneakers. "Is that chicken manure?"

"Yeah," Dougie said. "I had to go into the chicken coop to collect the eggs this morning."

Arful closed his eyes and sniffed again. "Ah, chicken is the best. The best! It has a rich, full aroma with bright overtones. It's my favorite thing to roll in next to dead fish."

Dougie laughed. "How often do you run into a dead fish around here?"

Arful sighed. "Not often enough."

"All right, you guys," Brian snapped. "Get serious. The girls will be over there any minute. Arful, you have to remember not to say anything."

Arful raised an eyebrow. "Even if somebody asks me a question?"

"*Especially* if somebody asks you a question!" Brian yelled. "You can't let on about knowing how to talk. You're there to listen and gather information."

Dougie snorted. "You going to have him take the notebook?"

Brian shot Dougie a look and called Arful over to the window. "That's where you're going. See the little pink playhouse with the purple curtains?"

"Yup."

"Just go over and wait until the girls arrive. You have to look cute so they let you in. And remember—no talking! No matter what happens, you don't say a word."

It took about ten minutes to coax Arful down the ladder. He was much better at climbing up than going down. Then we sent him off and went back into the treehouse to watch. He took his place beside the playhouse, and a few minutes later we saw him wag his tail when the girls showed up.

"Perfect timing," Brian said.

"You think they'll let him in?" I asked. My question was answered when Cara leaned down to pet him, then let him follow her into the playhouse.

Brian wrote something in his notebook, then closed it, smiling. "Operation Dog Spy has begun."

chapter 7

All right. I'm sitting here right by the small pink house, waiting, just like Brian said. I'm supposed to look cute, but I'm not sure what that is. I think it's when I perk up one ear. Brian's mother likes it when I do that. She always laughs and gives me extra dog biscuits.

My right ear is getting tired. I'll switch to the left one. Oh-oh. Here they come. They look friendly, even the nasty one from the park. Whoo-ee, they smell bad, though. You'd think they'd know enough to roll in something rotten once in a while. They should teach that in school. That's one of the first things a mother dog teaches her pups.

"Well, look at this." The one that smells like roses has a high little voice. Geez! Hurts my ears. "Aren't you cute?" I want to tell her I'm cute because of my perky ear, but I guess she knows that. Anyway, I'm not supposed to say anything.

"That's Brian Lewis's dog," Peppermint Breath says. She reaches down and scratches my ears. I like that, but the peppermint burns my eyes.

Then the nasty one comes out carrying a big bowl. What was her name? Emily? She smells like—food!

"Go on in," Emily says. "I have the potato chips, but I couldn't find any dip."

Dip! Glad she couldn't find that! I have to have dip every month during the summer to kill my fleas. Yuck! I follow the girls into the playhouse.

I discover that Peppermint Breath has the lovely smell of a sweaty baseball glove on her right hand, so I settle in at her feet and lick up the potato chip crumbs as they fall.

"We have to come up with something wonderful," Emily says. "There's no way we're letting those boys win."

"Why did you tell them they could order us around one whole week in school?" Peppermint Breath whines. "What if we lose?"

"We won't lose, Cara. If you and Lissa do just as I say, we'll win for sure." Emily takes a big handful

of chips and spills half of them on the floor. I love when that happens. They barely hit the ground before I snarf them up.

So now I figure out that Peppermint Breath is called Cara and the one that smells like roses is Lissa. Funny names. I'll have to remember those names to tell Brian. I'm sure that's important. He's going to be proud of me.

Lissa doesn't look happy. If she were a dog, she'd be growling, but she just speaks in her normal voice. "Why do you always get to be the boss?"

"Because I have the best ideas," Emily says. "I think we should do a dance—a ballet."

"Dance!" Lissa cries. "You're the only one who knows how to dance. And ballet is the hardest kind of dance there is."

Emily takes some chips but doesn't spill a crumb. I hate when that happens. "Don't worry. I'll teach you."

I smell a chipmunk. It must be just outside the playhouse. I'd like to go chase it, but Brian will be mad if I leave the meeting. They're still talking.

Just then a lady knocks on the door and comes in. The playhouse is too short for her to stand all the way up. She starts to say something, but then she sees me. "Where did this dog come from?"

"He belongs to a boy in our class, Mom. He lives over on the next street."

"Oh," she says. "Well, isn't he cute."

I want to tell her I'm not cute because I don't have either of my ears perked, but her face says she doesn't really think I'm cute anyway. I don't smell any biscuits on her, so there's no reason to start ear-perking now.

"I'm sorry to break up your meeting, but Emily has to go to the dentist now," the lady says.

Emily makes a face. I wonder what the dentist is? Maybe it's like going to the veterinarian. After the girls pack up their stuff and go out, the lady watches to make sure I leave the yard.

She's not a dog person. A dog can always tell.

34

chapter

I was the first one to spot Arful coming back from Emily's.

"Something's wrong," Brian said. "They must have kicked him out."

"Everything's fine," I said. "Look. Emily's mother is just pulling out of the driveway. She's taking Emily somewhere. The meeting's over."

We all scrambled down the ladder to meet Arful.

"Well," Brian asked, "what did you find out?"

"Lots of stuff," Arful said. "Important stuff. There are three of them. The one that smells like roses is named Lissa. Then there's Cara. She plays baseball. And the nasty one is named Emily."

Brian was just staring at his dog.

"You know which one I mean," Arful continued. "The one from the park? That's Emily."

"I know that's Emily," Brian said, "and I know the names of the others, too. I've been going to school with them since kindergarten, for Pete's sake. Didn't you find out anything else? Anything important?"

Arful let his ears droop. "Names are important."

Dougie sat on the ground next to Arful and put

his arm around the dog's neck. "It's okay, buddy. What else did you find out?"

Arful perked up. "I know that Lissa had a tuna sandwich for lunch. Her hands smelled so delicious, I wanted to lick them. And Cara has a cat at home. Smelled like a Siamese to me although it might have been one of those weird new breeds. Anyway, it's something with short hair, and—"

"This is not important stuff!" Brian yelled. "Didn't you hear anything about what they're doing for the talent show?"

Arful lay down and put his head between his paws. "Well, I heard something, but if you're going to get mad at me for every little mistake, I won't tell you."

I reached down to pet Arful. "Nobody's mad at you, Arful. Just try to think about what they said."

"There was a word I didn't know. Dallay or sallay." Arful's eyes were sad. "I don't remember anything else."

Brian sat down beside him. "Just think a little harder, Arful. Can you remember another word?"

Arful was thinking so hard the skin on his forehead wrinkled. "Well, there was something like ants. That's wasn't the word, though."

"Was it pants?" I asked. "Plants? Slants?"

Arful just kept shaking his head.

"France!" Dougie said.

"That's stupid," Brian said. "France isn't spelled anything like ants."

Dougie glared at him. "Who cares how it's spelled? The words sound the same. Besides those dallay or sally words sound like French, so maybe it was France."

Arful perked up. "France. Yup. I think that's it. France."

Brian hit himself on the side of the head. "Wait a minute. It wasn't sallay. It was soufflé, right, Arful?"

"Yup again. Sure sounds like it."

Brian wrote something in his notebook, then closed it with a snap. "That's it. They're doing French cooking."

"Cooking?" Arful asked, getting more interested. "You mean like cooking food?"

"Who does cooking for a talent show?" I asked. "That's the stupidest thing I ever heard."

Brian pushed his glasses up on his nose. "For your information, I saw a contestant in the Miss Teen Scene beauty pageant use cooking for her talent. If it's good enough for a national competition on TV, it's good enough for Percival Hatch Elementary School."

I wasn't going to argue with him. Brian watched more TV than any kid I knew. If he said cooking was a talent, then I believed him.

"Now," Brian said. "All we have to do is practice making a soufflé. There's not enough time to do it now, so you guys come over here tomorrow after school and we'll work in our kitchen."

chapter

9

We're in the kitchen, my favorite place in the whole house. I pride myself on keeping this floor licked spotless. I'm hoping for a lot of spilling, because these guys haven't a clue how to cook. I settle in the corner that gives me the best view. I could spot a dropped sesame seed from here.

"Okay," Brian says, reading from a book. "We only have four days to become soufflé experts. Josh, get a cup of flour from that canister. Dougie, we need eight eggs."

"Eight eggs coming up," Dougie says, opening the refrigerator. He lines up four eggs on the counter. While he goes back for more, I'm watching the one that's starting to roll toward the edge. Rolling . . . rolling . . . splat! I'm there! Thank you, Dougie!

"Hey!" Brian yells. "Watch what you're doing. Mom will have a fit if we make a mess."

"You can't even tell anything spilled," Dougie says. "Look. Arful cleaned it up already."

"Are you sure your mother doesn't mind us doing this?" Josh asked. He had measured out a cup of flour. A lot of it was on his shirt.

"I told her it's a school project. Besides, Dad's working in his study. He'll help if we get in any trouble. Now, it says to separate the eggs."

"Okay." Dougie moves the eggs farther apart from each other on the counter. "Do you think they're separated far enough?"

I'm watching for another roller. No luck so far, but a dog can hope.

Brian scratches his head. "It doesn't say. I don't know why that's important anyway."

"Probably just gives you more room to work," Josh says.

Brian nods. "Right. Okay, next step. Beat egg whites until stiff but not dry." He breaks an egg into a bowl.

"How do you get the yolk out of the white?" Josh asks.

"Easy," Brian says. He takes out a big spoon and fishes around in the bowl. "Oops."

"You wrecked it," Dougie says. "Let me try one with my fingers." He cracks another egg into the bowl. "Oops."

"Do you think it matters?" Josh asks. "Whites and yolks are all part of an egg."

"They wouldn't say beat the whites unless it mattered," Brian says.

"I bet that's what they meant by separating the eggs," Dougie says. "You were supposed to separate the whites from the yolks."

"I could get those yolks out of there for you," I offer, after they goof up three more eggs. "I can suck the insides out of a quail egg without crushing the shell. That's delicate work."

Brian shrugs. "You can't do any worse than we have." He breaks the rest of the eggs into the bowl and puts it on the floor.

I want to lap up the whole thing, but I keep telling myself, "Just the yolks, Arful. Just the yolks." When I finish, there are only a few streaks of yolk left from the eggs the boys messed up. I don't break a single one. I just get my doggy lips around each of those yolks and inhale real slow and easy. I'm so good, I could be a chef.

Brian picks up the bowl. "Not bad. Let's beat

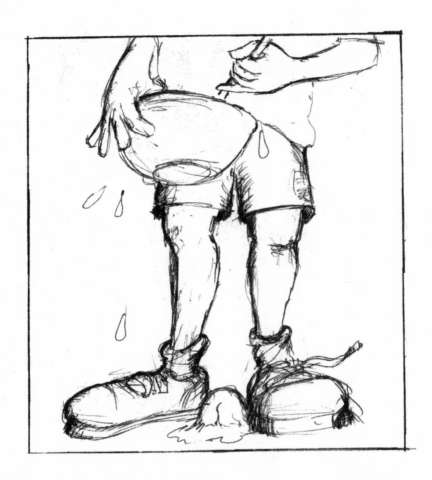

them." He turns on the mixer, with Josh and Dougie hanging over his shoulders. He beats for a long time.

"They're not getting stiff," Dougie says.

I stand and put my paws on the counter so I can see. Now the eggs look like white soupy oatmeal. "They're stiffer than they were," I say, trying not to drool into the bowl. I do love eggs.

Brian turns off the beater. "That's good enough. Now it says to fold the egg whites into the yolk and cheese mixture. Hey! We were supposed to save the yolks?"

"Too late now," Dougie says. "We'll wing it. I'll get the cheese."

"We can't wing it," Brian says. "We have to follow the recipe."

Dougie grabs a hunk of cheese from the refrigerator and puts it on the counter. "We're already winging it. It doesn't say to have your dog suck the yolks out of the egg whites, does it?" He dumps the goopy egg whites over the hunk of cheese.

"What are you doing?" Brian yells.

"Leave me alone. I'm folding!" Dougie tries to bring the goop up over the cheese, but it keeps sliding off.

"Wait," Josh says. "There was supposed to be flour in this thing. Maybe that will make it stiffer." He tries to dump the flour over the egg-cheese thing, but Brian pushes him out of the way. Then Dougie shoves Brian, and everything lands on the floor. It's a beautiful sight.

"Is it ruined?" I ask hopefully.

Brian sighs. "Of course it's ruined. Look at the mess we've made."

"Don't worry. I'll clean up." I start lapping at it. I

44

save the beaters and the mixer bowl for last. When I finish, you'd never know that mixer had been used. I nudge it back into its place and lick that counter until it sparkles.

The boys come back into the room just as I'm finishing up the floor.

"Wow," Dougie says. "Nice work, Arful!"

"Thanks," I say. I can't understand why humans hate cleaning. I think it's delicious.

Brian gets down next to me. "Now listen, Arful. The girls will probably have another meeting to-morrow and we're going to send you in to spy again.

This time, listen to what they're saying, and watch carefully how they make the soufflé. There must be a trick to it. You have to find out what it is, because we're running out of time. Tomorrow is Friday and the talent show is Monday night."

Here I am on my second spy mission. I'm going to get it right this time. I remember what Brian said. Listen and watch.

Here come the girls. They like me. I don't even have to perk my ears to get a smile. They let me right into the playhouse. I curl up on the floor in a spot of sunlight and start listening and watching.

"All right," Emily says. "We wasted a whole meeting yesterday not coming up with anything. I have a new idea. I think we should . . ."

The sun is warm and feels so good on my coat. I stretch and roll over on my other side. I'm in a big meadow and there are bunnies hopping all over the place. I love to chase bunnies almost as much as cats. I'm running after them and I'm leaping over . . . I'm not listening! I'm asleep!

I sit up and shake the sleep out of my head. Words. I have to listen to the words. I go sit by Cara and try to keep my eyes wide open.

"I don't think we'll win any contest with that plan," Cara says.

She starts scratching behind my ears, just the way I like it. It's hard to sit on the slippery floor, because my feet keep sliding out from under me. "You want to come up on the couch with me, Arful? Come on, it's all right."

I jump up and settle in next to her. She's still scratching. It feels wonderful.

Emily's talking again. "This is my final plan. We all need to go home and get . . . yada yada yada yada . . . Then we'll bring them back here and make yada yada yada . . ."

Nice scratching. Nice words. Nice sunshine.

chapter

10

When Arful came back from his spy mission at Emily's Friday afternoon, we went into Brian's living room. That's when we found out he hadn't learned anything.

"What do you mean, you slept!" Brian cried. "You wasted the whole meeting? We don't know if they'll have another one before the talent show. That could've been our last chance! How could you sleep through it?"

Arful circled about sixteen times before he lay down on the couch. "I couldn't help it." He yawned. "You humans don't put any excitement in your talk—no howling, no barking, no yelping. Just mumble, mumble, mumble. Sheesh! It's a wonder you don't put each other to sleep."

"You must have seen something," Brian insisted. "Think, Arful. We only have the weekend now. Were they making soufflé?"

"A what?"

"A soufflé! The thing we were trying to cook yesterday."

"There was no cooking. I would have remembered that."

"Aha!" Brian said. "They must have given up on the soufflé. It was too hard for them. So what kind of an act did they come up with? Did they have any props? Or costumes?"

"What are costumes?" Arful asked.

"Clothes," I offered. "They might have special clothes for the contest."

"Oh." Arful blinked. "They had pieces of cloth covering their bodies, the things humans wear. Which reminds me of something I've always wondered about. Why do humans keep changing their outer coat all at once? It's much easier to just shed it a little bit at a time, you know."

"The costumes, Arful." Brian moved closer to get his attention. "Were they in dresses? Pants?"

Arful thought for a minute. "No, they were

breathing normally. It was quite cool and pleasant in their playhouse."

"Not pants like breathing hard! Pants! Jeans!" Brian lifted one leg, shaking it for emphasis.

"Oh, I see what you mean," Arful said. "They probably have a special room for that, just like you do."

"What are you talking about?" Brian asked.

"The bat room," Arful said. "Why do you call it that? I've never sniffed any evidence of bats in the bat room."

"That's *bath*room," I said. "It doesn't have anything to do with bats."

Arful perked up one ear. "I know you humans sometimes go into that room to take a bath, but it seems you use it more for leaving messages. Why do you leave all of your messages in one little bowl inside the house? You could reach so many more people by leaving a message on the tree in the front yard. That's what I do, and I get answers from dogs all over town. There was a dog the other day from Cleveland. Can you imagine? He said his family had moved away and he was following them."

"You get all that from sniffing a tree?" I asked.

Dougie was rolling around the floor, laughing, at this point. "We get e-mail; Arful gets p-mail!"

Arful perked up his ears. "Exactly. By the way, now that I'm learning more of your words, I'm curious about my name. What does Arful mean?"

"Well, the 'arf' part is from a dog bark," Brian said.

"Arf?" Arful looked puzzled. "Who says arf? I never said 'arf' in my whole life."

Brian shrugged. "Sorry. That's what it sounds like when you bark."

Arful put his head between his paws and raised one eyebrow. "I keep forgetting that human hearing is so primitive. We're actually saying 'aroov,' which means 'Heads up! Here comes the mailman.' But that still doesn't explain my whole name."

Brian looked to me. I knew he didn't want to be the one to hurt Arful's feelings. "It's sort of a joke," I offered. "It sounds like 'awful,' which is the way you looked when they got you from the shelter." It was the way he still looked, but I didn't say that.

Arful raised his head and smiled. "I like that. Awful—Arful. A name with a joke. Could we change it to Aroovful, though?"

Brian shook his head. "I don't think so. It would be hard to remember."

Arful sighed and put his head on his paws again. "I'm learning a whole new language here. You can't remember one new word?"

"Okay," I said. "How about we leave the name

the same, but every time we see the mailman, we'll yell 'aroov'?"

Arful perked up. "That's a deal. It's 'arooz' for garbage collectors, and 'aroosh' for salesmen, just in case you spot any of those while I'm napping. I hate to miss a chance to chase away invaders."

chapter
11

It's Saturday. We're up in the treehouse, watching Emily's backyard. We've been watching all day, and nobody's showing up.

"I was afraid of this," Brian says. "They must have gotten suspicious. I bet they're practicing at somebody else's house where we can't spy on them."

"Maybe they're just goofing off this weekend," Josh says. "Maybe they gave up on the whole thing, which I think, by the way, is a great idea."

Brian shakes his head. "Emily is not a goof-off, and she never gives up. She probably has them practicing their brains out. They must be practically professional by now. We're doomed."

Dougie has his head in an empty bag of chips, trying to lick the salt and crumbs from the bottom. "I don't know why it's so important to know what the girls are doing anyway."

"It's important because that's how we figure out how to do something better," Brian says, rolling his eyes. "I've explained that about a hundred times. Why don't you listen for a change?"

"Look," Dougie says, coming up for air without spilling a crumb, "it doesn't matter what the girls do. We'll be better. We have a sure-fire act."

"What act?" Brian cries. "We have nothing!"

"Now who's not listening? I told you before. We have Arful."

"And I told you before, I don't want anybody finding out that my dog can talk."

"That's the beauty of my plan. Nobody will find out. Arful, come over here."

I trot over to Dougie, and he whispers in my ear. It tickles. "Okay, Arful, do you understand what we're going to do?"

"Sure," I say. "I mean I sort of . . . I have an idea . . . well . . . actually, no. Haven't a clue."

"All right. Listen carefully." This time Dougie lifts my ear to whisper in it. This tickles even more than the last time. But this time I know what he wants me to do.

"Okay," Dougie says. "Let's try it. You ready, Arful?"

"Yup."

Dougie gives me the signal.

"Hi, I'm Arful the talking dog. I can talk and I can tell jokes."

"What are you doing?" Brian yells. "I said I don't want anybody to know he talks."

"That's what makes this so cool," Dougie says. "Nobody will know he's talking. We'll say I'm a ventriloquist."

"But it doesn't look like you're talking," Josh says. "Your lips aren't even moving."

Dougie rolls his eyes. I think he learned that from Brian. "My lips aren't supposed to be moving. A ventriloquist doesn't move his lips."

"But they're not going to believe that you're really doing the talking unless you move your lips a little," Brian says.

Dougie grins. "What do you think they're going to think? You think they're going to think the dog is talking? I don't think so."

Dougie may look dumb, but sometimes he has more common sense than Brian and Josh put together.

"Oh." Brian scratches his head. "I see what you mean. Maybe this'll work after all. All we need to do is teach Arful some jokes, then decide which one of us should be the ventriloquist."

"Hey, I was the one who thought up the idea," Dougie says. "I get to be the ventriloquist."

"It's all yours," Josh says. "I want to be as far away from that auditorium as possible."

Brian nods. "That sounds fair, I guess. But there has to be something for Josh and me to do. After all, we're all supposed to be entering the talent show together."

Josh backs away. "Hey, you can leave me out of this. I don't need to be up on that stage again. The last time was enough."

Brian keeps going. "You're a good artist, Josh. We need a big sign. You could make one and then hold it. And somebody has to pretend they're making Arful's lips move. I'll do that, because he's used to me. He might bite you."

That hurt my feelings. I'd never bite Josh. Brian knows me better than that. If I can't eat it, I don't bite it. Well, except for a stick. But that's just a game.

chapter
12

We spent all day Sunday in Brian's room while Dougie tried to teach Arful some jokes. He insisted he had to do it himself if he was going to be the ventriloquist. It practically killed Brian not to be in charge, but we both sat on his bed and didn't open our mouths.

"Let's start out with the knock-knock joke," Dougie said. "Knock-knock."

Arful just looked at him.

"Arful, you're supposed to say 'Who's there?'."

"Who's where?"

"Here. It doesn't matter where. Just say 'Who's there?'"

"Who's there or who's here? It's not the same thing. Besides, I know who's here and I don't know where there is."

Dougie hit himself in the forehead. "Okay, Arful. Forget the knock-knocks. Why did the chicken cross the road?"

Arful blinked. "The chicken crossed the road when it smelled something really interesting across the street?"

"No! That's not it, Dougie said. "I just told you the answer two minutes ago."

"Well, that's why I would cross the road . . .

carefully, of course." Arful's eyes brightened. "Ooh! Ooh! I know. To chase the cat who lived across the street."

"No! Chickens don't chase cats. Chickens cross the road to get to the other side."

Arful raised his head. "And then what do they do?"

"Nothing! That's the joke!"

"Oh." Arful put his head down again. "That's not funny. How about we use one of my jokes? Why does a cat cross the road?"

Dougie sighed. "I don't know. Why?"

"To get away from the dog who's chasing him. Now *that's* funny." Arful jumped to his feet. "I've got another one. How many cats does it take to screw in a lightbulb?"

"How many?" we all chimed in.

"None. Cats don't need lightbulbs. They can see in the dark." Arful laughed at his own joke, a low woofy sound. "Why did the dog chase the cat?"

"Why?"

"To get a little catnip. Get it? The dog nips the cat?" He slapped his belly with a paw. "I got a million of 'em."

"You know," Brian said, "as stupid as these jokes are, they're funny because they're the kind of jokes a dog would think up."

"Well, duh! A dog did think them up," I said.

Arful was on a roll now. "What kind of bag does a doggy bring home from a restaurant?"

Dougie sighed. "I give. What kind of bag?"

Arful snorted. "A people bag. Get it? People get doggy bags. Doggies get people bags."

We all groaned. But I had to admit, Arful had a better act than any of us could have come up with. And since the talent show was tomorrow night, we were out of time.

chapter
13

They're taking me to school again. I wonder what I'll learn this time?

It's so crowded in here I can't see faces, only legs. Most of them have that awful soapy smell they get from taking baths and showers. I just can't understand why humans do that. They smell just fine the way they are, especially kids after they've been playing outside all day.

Some bald guy is telling my kids we have to wait in the music room until he comes to get us. Get us for what? I wish somebody would tell me what's going on, but I can't ask. On the way here, Brian told me about six times not to talk to anybody, no matter how much I wanted to say something.

I smell fear. Brian is sweating and it's not even hot in here. I give a little low growl in my throat, just in case the thing he's afraid of is nearby.

Here comes that man who told us where to wait. "All right, boys. Come with me. You're going to wait in the wings for the next two acts, then you're on."

I can sense that Brian is afraid of something. So is Josh. I growl at the man. He backs off. "You'll have to keep that dog quiet. Is he vicious?"

Brian grabs my collar. I hate when he does that. "Arful wouldn't hurt anybody, Mr. Purvis."

I want to say I'll hurt whatever my kids are afraid of, but I'm not supposed to talk. I try to hold the kids back, blocking their way, but Brian and Josh both grab the leash and pull me. I try to dig in my nails, but the floors are slippery as ice.

"Here's where you wait," the man whispers. "Now be quiet."

I look around. This is that same stage we were on at the Science Fair. I smell fear. It's even stronger here. I break the no-talking rule. "Why are you afraid?"

Brian drops to his knees with a hammerlock on my head. "Shhhhh!"

I struggle to get loose. "Who are you afraid of?" I whisper. Well, it's a little louder than that. Dogs aren't great at whispering.

"It's nothing," Brian says. "Just a little stage fright."

There's a boy out on the stage, talking now. He's waving his arms around.

"Lester Borton is going to put the whole audience to sleep," Josh whispers.

"Shakespeare," Brian says. "Why didn't we think of that? We could have had Arful reciting Shakespeare."

Dougie snorts. "He can't even remember knock-knock jokes and you're going to teach him Shakespeare?"

Dougie is wrong. I can remember knock-knock jokes.

Knock-knock.

Who's there?

Me and Dougie and Josh and Brian.

And some kid out on the stage waving his arms around.

That's who's here.

So there!

chapter
14

Lester Borton finally finished his Shakespeare thing.
There was a lot of applause, then the next act came
out. It was Emily, Lissa, and Cara dressed in gold
costumes so sparkly they practically blinded us.

"Sequins," whispered Brian. "Why didn't we
think of that?"

"No way you'd ever get me to wear sequins," I
hissed.

Each of the girls was holding a silver baton, and
when Emily gave the signal, they started twirling.
It was easy to see that Emily was the only one
who knew what she was doing. Lissa and Cara were
faking it, but made up for their lack of skill by

doing a lot of smiling, kicking, and spinning around. Then they all threw the batons up in the air. Emily spun around three times and caught hers perfectly. Cara and Lissa bumped into each other and Lissa's baton clobbered Cara on the head. Then Cara missed hers and it came bouncing toward our side of the stage.

"Stick!" Arful shouted. "Wanna play stick?" He broke loose, lunged for the baton, and picked it up in his mouth, which was a good thing, because it kept him from saying anything else. He bounded out on the stage and took the baton to Cara. As soon as she reached for it, he ducked out of her reach and started running in circles around them. That was Arful's version of the stick game. He'd get it away from you, then run around until he got tired.

I grabbed Brian's arm. "You gotta go out there and get your dog."

"Are you kidding? Emily would beat my brains out with that baton. I'm not going near her."

Arful dropped Cara's baton in the back corner of the stage, and swooped by Lissa to grab hers before she knew what was happening. Then he went back and snarfed up Cara's baton and carried the two of them up to the front of the stage. The audience went

wild as he pranced in front of Emily with the two
silver sticks in his mouth.

Lissa and Cara were cracking up, but Emily's
phony smile disappeared and she showed her true
personality right in front of the whole school. She

lunged for Arful, but he moved too fast for her. She landed flat on the stage, and Arful grabbed her baton to add to the others. The audience roared. It sounded like the winning touchdown at a football game.

Emily went into a full-scale tantrum, kicking and pounding the floor with her fists, while Arful galloped around her in a big circle. The three batons stretched his mouth into a wide grin.

Cara and Lissa pulled themselves together, and hauled Emily to her feet. They bowed and dragged her off our side of the stage with Arful following, tail held high and wagging.

"I'll never forgive you for this, Brian Lewis," Emily gasped. "You made your dog ruin our act on purpose. And now I have icky dog slobber all over my baton."

"I didn't do anything," Brian said. "Honest! He just ran out on his own."

"I heard you yell to him to go play stick."

"That wasn't me. That was—"

I jabbed Brian hard with my elbow, although if I'd let him say it was Arful, nobody would have believed him anyway.

"If you win now, it doesn't count," Emily cried. "It doesn't count because you cheated! The bet is off."

Cara grabbed the batons while Arful wasn't paying attention. Lissa pulled Emily away from Brian.

Brian clutched his stomach. "I think I'm going to be sick. Josh, you be the one to make Arful's lips move."

"But who's going to hold the sign?"

"Forget the sign." Brian turned and threw up on Mr. Purvis's shoes.

chapter
15

I'm not sure, but I think I goofed. Emily just called me some bad names, and Brian got sick and ran off. I don't understand what I did wrong. I only played stick the way I always do. It wasn't easy either, because these sticks were hard and slippery. I couldn't even dig my teeth into them.

"Come on, Arful." Josh has me by the collar and is pulling me back out on that stage. I'm going to stop wearing a collar if everybody insists on using it to drag me around.

I don't see any sticks. This must be a new game. I'm going to stay out of trouble this time, though. I try to remember everything I've ever been told not to do. "Don't get on the couch." I look around. That's easy, there's no couch here.

"Don't snitch food from the table." Check. No table, no snitching. Looks like I'm in pretty good shape here.

Dougie goes to the front of the stage. "Ladies and gentlemen, here is Arful, the amazing talking dog." He looks over at me. "Say hello, Arful."

I just remembered another no-no. "Don't talk in public. Don't say a word to anybody. Keep your big doggy mouth shut." How many times have I heard that? So this is a trick. Dougie is trying to make me talk in public, but I'm too smart to fall for that. I clamp my jaws tight and don't say a word.

"That's your cue, Arful," Josh whispers in my ear. "Remember your line? 'I'm Arful the talking dog'? C'mon! Don't just sit there. Say something!"

This is a bigger test than I thought. Two against one. That's not fair, but I'm smart. And I'm not talking.

Dougie comes over and squats in front of me. "Don't be scared, Arful. Just do it the way we practiced. Remember the jokes? You can tell your own jokes. Anything you want. We'll start with your knock-knock."

He turns to the audience. "Arful is the world's only dog comedian. He's going to tell you a dog knock-knock joke. Go ahead, Arful."

Not saying a word. Not me. No sir.

Suddenly Josh grabs my lower jaw and makes my mouth move up and down while he says, "Knock-knock," in a low gruff voice.

"Who's there?" Dougie asks.

"Olive."

Olive? I don't even like olives. I clamp my jaw even tighter so all Josh gets to move is the skin around my lower lip.

"Olive who?"

"Olive you."

That's the dumbest joke I ever heard. The kids in the audience are groaning.

Dougie gives me a weird look. Then he says, "Why does the chicken cross the road?"

They're back to the stupid chicken again? "The chicken crosses the road to get to the other side," Josh says. He grips my jaw and tries to make it look like my mouth is moving while he talks. Hey, that's not fair. It's bad enough that they're trying to make me talk in public. But now they're making me look dumb by telling these really lame jokes.

"How many dogs does it take to screw in a lightbulb?" Dougie asks.

That does it. It's my joke and he can't even get the first line right. When Josh tries to grab my jaw again, I open my mouth and clamp down on his hand. I'm not biting. Just holding. Josh lets out a yell.

All of a sudden the short bald guy comes running out on the stage. "You stop that right now." He grabs me by the collar. I am so sick of people using my collar as a handle.

"Hey, cut it out, Baldy!" I yell.

The bald guy looks at Josh. "What did you say, young man?"

chapter
16

I just sat there on the stage looking up at Mr. Purvis while he held Arful by the collar.

"I mean it, Baldy," Arful said. "Let go of the collar."

Mr. Purvis's jaw dropped. "Did he just . . . ? Did I hear . . . ?" The way he was looking at Arful, I knew he was going to blurt it right out in front of the whole school about Arful talking. He was the only one close enough to tell where the sound was coming from.

In a split second I went from Josh Buckner, quiet kid who nobody ever notices, to Josh Buckner, juvenile delinquent. "You heard me, Baldy," I growled in a low voice like Arful's. "Let the dog go."

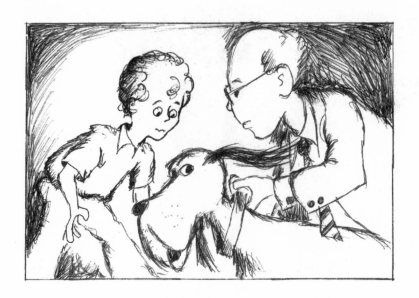

Mr. Purvis's eyes narrowed. "You and your parents will be in my office first thing tomorrow morning. Is that understood?"

"You're not a nice person," Arful said. "I don't like you."

I grabbed Arful and clamped my hand over his muzzle.

Mr. Purvis motioned for the curtains to close. "You're only making things harder on yourself, Josh."

Dougie came running over to us. "What happened? We're not finished."

"Oh, you're finished, all right," Mr. Purvis said. "And don't bother coming back onto the stage for the judging. You're disqualified."

The curtain opened again and Mr. Purvis called everybody but us back on the stage.

Lester got a lot of applause for his Shakespeare act, but when Emily, Lissa, and Cara came out, the place went nuts. "Where's the dog?" somebody yelled. Then they started chanting, "We want the dog! We want the dog!"

"Do they mean me?" Arful asked.

Dougie patted his head. "Who else? Go out there and take a bow."

When Arful pranced up to the girls, Cara gave him her baton and he made a big circle around them, his tail wagging like a victory flag. There was no question about it, Emily's act got ten times more applause than anybody else.

Just then Brian came back. He still looked a little green. "How did it go?"

I didn't know how even to start explaining what had happened, so I just shook my head.

"They're voting now. Why aren't you guys out there?"

"Don't ask," Dougie said.

Mr. Purvis handed Emily the trophy. They all took another bow, then Arful bounded back to us in the wings. "They liked me! They really liked me!"

Emily was just far enough behind him that she

hadn't heard. "Get ready to follow orders for a whole week, Brian. We won, you lost."

"We didn't lose," Dougie said. "We were disqualified." The way he said it, you would've thought it was some kind of honor.

"What did you say to Mr. Purvis anyway, Josh?" Cara asked. "He looked really mad."

They hadn't heard? That was a relief. I was still in a heap of trouble, but at least the whole school didn't know I had called the principal "Baldy."

"You didn't win the bet," Brian said, "because you called it off when you thought Arful had ruined your act. So the deal is off."

Cara reached down to scratch Arful behind the ear. "Arful didn't ruin our act. He made us win. Now nobody gets to order anybody around. It turned out well for all of us."

Everybody but me, that is. I couldn't explain to Mom and Dad what had happened without giving away Arful's secret. In the meeting Tuesday morning with Mr. Purvis, I answered most of their questions by saying "I dunno." They finally chalked it up to temporary insanity brought on by stage fright. And I was grounded for a month.

chapter
17

It's Saturday, the weekend after the talent show. Josh's parents are letting Brian, Dougie, and me visit him, but he can't leave the house because he's grounded. How stupid is that? If you want to be on the *ground,* you have to be *outside* the house. It's just another one of those human words that doesn't mean what it says.

"I'm really sorry about Arful getting you in trouble," Brian says. "And thanks for taking the blame and not giving away his secret. Dougie told me what happened."

My ears perk up. "Trouble? What kind of trouble?"

"You called the principal 'Baldy,' and he thought Josh was doing the talking," Dougie says.

"But I didn't know his name. When a dog doesn't know another dog, he greets him by a made-up name, something about the way he looks. You know, 'Red' for an Irish setter, 'Curly' for a poodle, 'Low-belly' for a dachshund. It's not an insult."

"Trust me, 'Baldy' is an insult," Josh says.

"Oh." I let my ears droop. "I didn't mean to cause trouble. I was only trying to do what you wanted me to. First you tell me not to talk. Then it's 'Say something, Arful,' then it's 'Don't talk, Arful.'" I flop on the rug and sigh. "Humans are so confusing."

"The whole problem is the fact that Arful can talk," Brian says. "We have to fix him so he can't."

I jump to my feet. "Fix me? Oh, no you don't! I'm not falling for that trick again."

Brian pats my head. "It's not an operation, Arful. The reason you can talk is that we hypnotized you. We can do the same thing to put you back to normal. It doesn't hurt."

"Oh, yeah?" I back toward the door. "That's what they told me last time. 'Oh, it won't hurt.' Do I look stupid or something?"

Dougie laughs. "Why would you want to fix it so Arful can't talk? I think he's great this way. Josh was right. We get to learn how a dog thinks. And besides, this is the first time Arful has gotten anybody into trouble."

"We'll take a vote," Brian said. "All in favor of hypnotizing Arful so he can't talk."

"Do I get to vote?" I ask.

"Sure," Brian says.

"I should get two votes, because I'm the one you're trying to change. Maybe three votes, so I'm equal to you guys." I figured I already had Dougie on my side, but it wouldn't hurt to have the extra votes.

"One vote," Brian says. "All in favor of hypnotizing Arful so he can't talk?"

"I have lots more to say. If I can't talk, you'll never know what it is."

"All in favor—"

"I have secrets," I say. "Important secrets that only a dog knows."

"—raise your hands."

We all look at each other. Nobody raises a hand. Or a paw.

Brian hugs me. "Okay, Arful. You get to talk, but only to us."

"That's what I was trying to do when I got into trouble."

They spend the next twenty minutes trying to explain to me what went wrong at the talent show.

"Do you understand now?" Brian asks.

"Well, yes. It was because I wasn't supposed to talk in public . . . except I really was because I was supposed to tell about the chicken going across the road and I . . . Nope, haven't a clue."

The kids all laugh. Even though I can talk, I still don't understand the way humans think. A lot of the things they do and say seem stupid to me, but maybe dogs just have more sense.

It must be hard to be human. They can't sniff the air and get twenty different scents that tell them who and what is in the neighborhood. They can't hear that cat who's trying to pussyfoot though the backyard without being discovered. Most humans will never know the thrill of a good cat or bunny chase.

I'm watching these kids right now, and it makes me sad to think of all the things they can't enjoy. But they seem happy enough, maybe because they have no idea what they're missing.

On the way home with Brian, I'm thinking I'm glad I can still human-talk. I've been storing up a bunch of questions to ask. Like why do they put food in the garbage can and let the garbage man take it away just as it's starting to get ripe? And when we go for rides in the car, why don't they hang their heads out of the window so they can feel their ears flapping in the breeze? And what's with those things called shoes? Don't they know how great it feels to run in bare paws? Very young humans seem to understand that, but they forget as they grow older.

"Hey, Arful! Wanna play stick?"

That's Brian. We've reached the park, and he's picked up a really nice stick. He's waving it the way he always does just before he throws it. I start yapping and jumping up and down the way I'm supposed to. Then he throws it and I race to catch it before it lands. I don't know why humans like this game, but all the kids are nuts about it.

The first running and catching part is fun, but then it gets boring. I'm supposed to get almost close enough for Brian to grab the stick, then I run off. That part always makes him laugh. Like right now. He almost had his hand on the stick, but I snatched it away. He's laughing his head off.

Now that I can talk, maybe I can teach him some better games—ones with more complicated rules. But for now I'll keep doing this until Brian gets tired. It's dumb game, but I don't mind. Sometimes a dog's gotta do what a dog's gotta do. If this makes Brian happy, then I'm happy, too.

After all, he is my very own boy.

About the Author

Mary Jane Auch always loved to draw. As a child, she filled countless notebooks with comic-strip adventures of princes, princesses, and ordinary people. She studied art at Skidmore College and worked as a textile designer in New York City after her graduation. She later studied occupational therapy at Columbia University and began a second career working with children with cerebral palsy. After starting her own family, she began writing for children and is now known for her hilarious picture books, comic middle grade novels and chapter books, and historical fiction. She and her husband, Herm Auch, have two grown children and live on a small farm near Rochester, New York.